# Historic Houses
# of New England
# Coloring Book

## A. G. SMITH

DOVER PUBLICATIONS, INC.
New York

# Acknowledgments

The publishers wish to thank the following for their cooperation in the creation of this book: p. 1: Prudence Crandall Museum; p. 2: The Antiquarian & Landmarks Society, Hartford, CT; p. 3: Connecticut Historical Commission, Hartford, CT; p. 4: Gillette Castle State Park; p. 5: The Mark Twain Memorial, Hartford, CT; p. 6: Eugene O'Neill Theater Center, Waterford, CT; pp. 7, 11, 15, 22: Society for the Preservation of New England Antiquities, 141 Cambridge Street, Boston, MA 02114 (617/227-3956); p. 8: Harriet Beecher Stowe House; p. 9: Maine Historical Society, Portland, ME; p. 10: Mr. Charles Homer Willauer; p. 12: John Greenleaf Whittier Home; p. 13: The Emily Dickinson Homestead; p. 14: Isabella Stewart Gardner Museum; p. 16: The Paul Revere Memorial Association, Boston, MA; p. 17: Longfellow National Historic Site; p. 18: The Trustees of Reservations, Beverly, MA; p. 19: Orchard House; p. 20: William Cullen Bryant Homestead; p. 21: Alden Kindred of America, Inc., Duxbury, MA; p. 23: Edith Wharton Restoration, Inc., Lenox, MA; p. 24: Nantucket Maria Mitchell Science Center, Nantucket, MA; p. 25: Berkshire County Historical Society, Pittsfield, MA; p. 26: U.S. Department of the Interior, National Park Service, Adams National Historic Site; p. 27: House of the Seven Gables; p. 28: Thornton W. Burgess Society, Sandwich, MA; p. 29: Chesterwood Museum Archives, Chesterwood, a Property of the National Trust for Historic Preservation, Stockbridge, MA; p. 30: Saint-Gaudens National Historic Site; p. 31: The Museum at Lower Shaker Village, Enfield, NH; p. 32: Robert Frost Place; p. 33: The National Society of the Colonial Dames of America in the State of New Hampshire, Portsmouth, NH; pp. 34, 35, 36: The Preservation Society of Newport County, Newport, RI; p. 37: The John Brown House; p. 38: The Gilbert Stuart Memorial, Inc., Saunderstown, RI; pp. 39, 43: Vermont Division for Historic Preservation, Montpelier, VT; p. 40: Friends of Hildene, Inc., Manchester, VT; p. 41: Middlebury College, Middlebury, VT; p. 42: The Park-McCullough House.

*Historic Houses of New England Coloring Book* is a new work, first published by Dover Publications, Inc., in 1993.

*International Standard Book Number*

*ISBN-13: 978-0-486-27167-5*
*ISBN-10: 0-486-27167-6*

Manufactured in the United States by RR Donnelley
27167611    2015
www.doverpublications.com

# Publisher's Note

New England has been an important center of American cultural and political life since European settlers first colonized the region during the seventeenth century. Although small in comparison to their western counterparts, the New England states are distinguished by their individual characters, geography and traditions.

The forty-three houses depicted in this volume represent some of New England's most historically and architecturally significant structures. These buildings range in age and style from simple Pilgrim cabins to the opulent mansions of the Gilded Age, and many are associated with great figures in numerous fields of endeavor from the American past.

This book can be used as a guidebook for touring the New England states. All of these houses are open to the public; however, some can only be viewed on a limited basis (please check before visiting).

The sequence is alphabetical by state, and then by locality within the state.

# The New England States, Showing Location of Houses in This Book

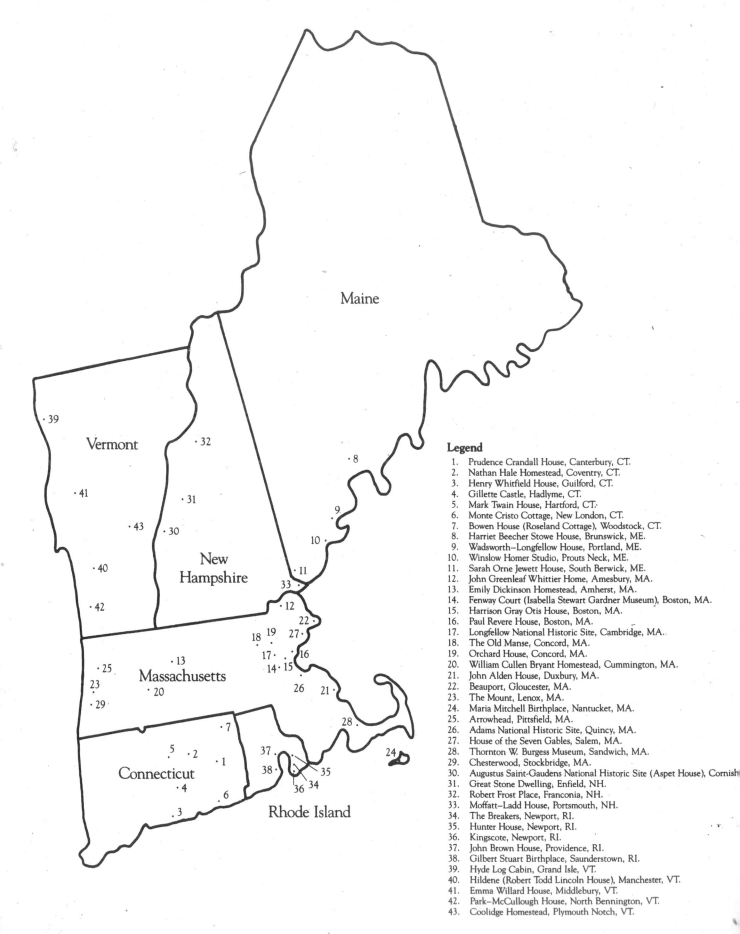

Maine

Vermont

· 39

· 41

· 43

· 40

· 42

New
Hampshire

· 32

· 31

· 30

· 8

· 9

10 ·

· 11

33 ·

· 12

22 ·

18 · 19  27 ·

17 · · 16

14 · 15

· 13

Massachusetts

· 25

23

· 20

· 29

26    21 ·

28 ·

· 7

5 ·  · 2

· 1

Connecticut

· 4    · 6

· 3

37 ·

38 ·

· 35

36  34

24 ·

Rhode Island

**Legend**

1. Prudence Crandall House, Canterbury, CT.
2. Nathan Hale Homestead, Coventry, CT.
3. Henry Whitfield House, Guilford, CT.
4. Gillette Castle, Hadlyme, CT.
5. Mark Twain House, Hartford, CT.
6. Monte Cristo Cottage, New London, CT.
7. Bowen House (Roseland Cottage), Woodstock, CT.
8. Harriet Beecher Stowe House, Brunswick, ME.
9. Wadsworth–Longfellow House, Portland, ME.
10. Winslow Homer Studio, Prouts Neck, ME.
11. Sarah Orne Jewett House, South Berwick, ME.
12. John Greenleaf Whittier Home, Amesbury, MA.
13. Emily Dickinson Homestead, Amherst, MA.
14. Fenway Court (Isabella Stewart Gardner Museum), Boston, MA.
15. Harrison Gray Otis House, Boston, MA.
16. Paul Revere House, Boston, MA.
17. Longfellow National Historic Site, Cambridge, MA.
18. The Old Manse, Concord, MA.
19. Orchard House, Concord, MA.
20. William Cullen Bryant Homestead, Cummington, MA.
21. John Alden House, Duxbury, MA.
22. Beauport, Gloucester, MA.
23. The Mount, Lenox, MA.
24. Maria Mitchell Birthplace, Nantucket, MA.
25. Arrowhead, Pittsfield, MA.
26. Adams National Historic Site, Quincy, MA.
27. House of the Seven Gables, Salem, MA.
28. Thornton W. Burgess Museum, Sandwich, MA.
29. Chesterwood, Stockbridge, MA.
30. Augustus Saint-Gaudens National Historic Site (Aspet House), Cornish
31. Great Stone Dwelling, Enfield, NH.
32. Robert Frost Place, Franconia, NH.
33. Moffatt–Ladd House, Portsmouth, NH.
34. The Breakers, Newport, RI.
35. Hunter House, Newport, RI.
36. Kingscote, Newport, RI.
37. John Brown House, Providence, RI.
38. Gilbert Stuart Birthplace, Saunderstown, RI.
39. Hyde Log Cabin, Grand Isle, VT.
40. Hildene (Robert Todd Lincoln House), Manchester, VT.
41. Emma Willard House, Middlebury, VT.
42. Park–McCullough House, North Bennington, VT.
43. Coolidge Homestead, Plymouth Notch, VT.

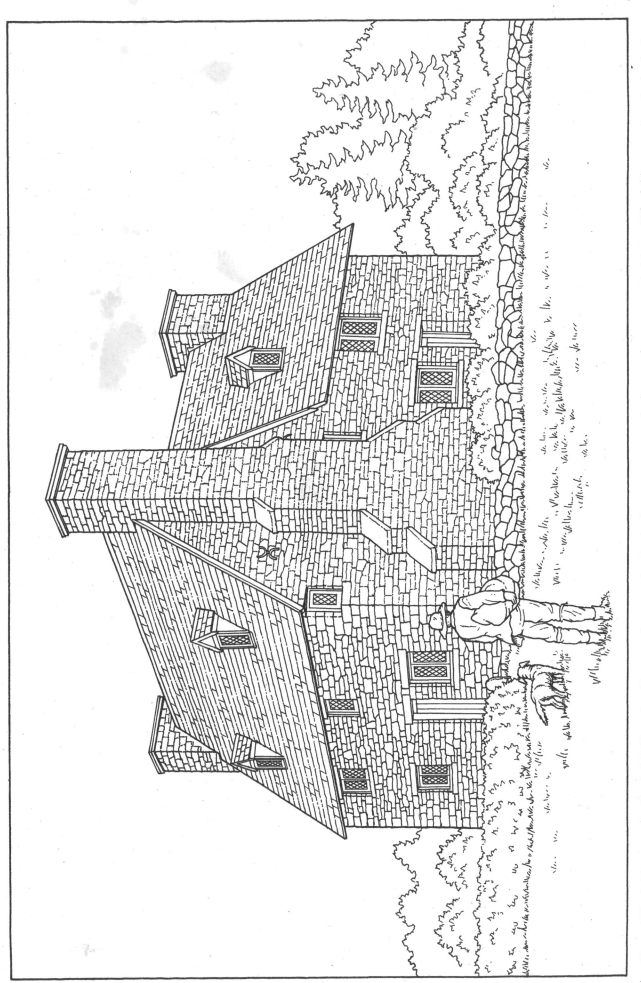

**3  Henry Whitfield House, Guilford, CT.** This, the oldest stone house in New England, was built in 1639–40 for Henry Whitfield, clergyman and leader of an early English settlement. The fortresslike structure was designed to serve both as a home for Whitfield and his large family and as a community refuge in the event of an Indian attack (a precaution which proved unnecessary). Master Whitfield returned to England after a decade; the house changed hands many times in the following centuries, and underwent major structural alterations. Purchased by the state in 1897, the building was subsequently restored and today serves as a museum recreating the early Colonial era.

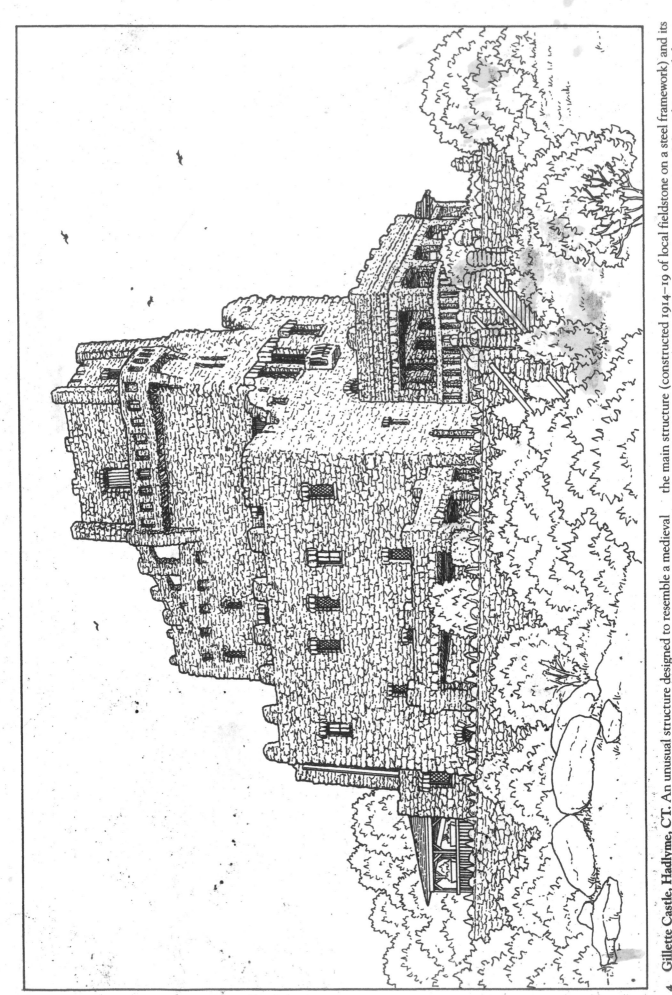

4 **Gillette Castle, Hadlyme, CT.** An unusual structure designed to resemble a medieval Rhenish fortress, sited overlooking the Connecticut River, Gillette Castle was the home of William Gillette, an actor and playwright best known as the star of his own theatrical adaptation of Sir Arthur Conan Doyle's Sherlock Holmes stories. Gillette designed both the main structure (constructed 1914–19 of local fieldstone on a steel framework) and its one-of-a-kind appointments, including many ingenious original furnishings and doors. Today operated as a museum by the state, the grounds also include carefully designed nature trails and a miniature railway built by the actor.

**5  Mark Twain House, Hartford, CT.** One of the most lavish residences of its day, this house was constructed in 1873–74 as the dwelling of author Mark Twain (Samuel Langhorne Clemens) and his family. An eccentric, sprawling amalgam of High Victorian Gothic and Stick Style elements, designed by New York architect Edward Tuckerman Potter, the structure reflects its owner's flamboyance and love of ornament. The equally opulent interior, wherein Clemens authored such classics as *Adventures of Huckleberry Finn*, includes decorative appointments by Louis Comfort Tiffany. Financial difficulties forced the Clemens family to leave the house, today restored as a museum, in 1891.

**6 Monte Cristo Cottage, New London, CT:** The boyhood summer home of playwright Eugene O'Neill, Monte Cristo Cottage was named by the dramatist's actor father after his most famous role—the lead in a stage adaptation of Dumas' *Le Comte de Monte Cristo*. The cottage was the only permanent home of the O'Neills, who spent much of the year on the road leading a precarious thespian life. A modest frame structure, the cottage has been immortalized as the setting of O'Neill's painfully autobiographical *Long Day's Journey Into Night* and, paradoxically, as the scene of his only comedy, *Ah, Wilderness!* Today the cottage is a museum devoted to O'Neill and his works.

**7  Bowen House (Roseland Cottage), Woodstock, CT.**
Roseland Cottage's unusual Gothic Revival design and pink walls stand in surprising contrast to its sedate Colonial surroundings. Constructed in 1846 for businessman and publisher Henry C. Bowen, the cottage was the work of architect Joseph Collins Wells, known mainly for his Gothic churches. The grounds include a nineteenth-century garden and one of the nation's oldest bowling alleys. A lavish host, Bowen entertained many notables of his day, including Presidents Grant, Hayes, Harrison and McKinley, at gala Independence Day celebrations. Today the cottage is a museum administered by the Society for the Preservation of New England Antiquities.

**8  Harriet Beecher Stowe House, Brunswick, ME.** In this building abolitionist Harriet Beecher Stowe, sister of noted clergyman and author Henry Ward Beecher, wrote her novel *Uncle Tom's Cabin.* Its harrowing depiction of the life of Southern slaves caused an immediate sensation upon publication in book format in 1852, and exerted an incalculable influence upon the North in the years before the Civil War (leading Abraham Lincoln to address Stowe as "the little lady who made the big war"). Constructed as an inn in 1804, the house was occupied by the author from 1850 to 1852, while her husband was teaching at nearby Bowdoin College. Today the site serves once more as an inn.

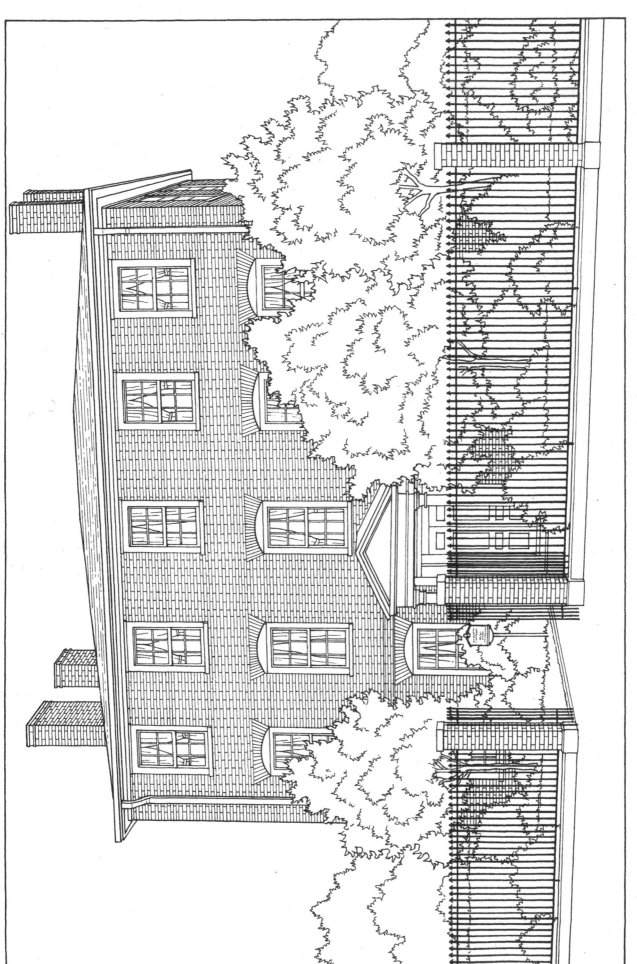

**9  Wadsworth–Longfellow House, Portland, ME.** The boyhood home of the most popular American poet of the nineteenth century, Henry Wadsworth Longfellow, this house was built in 1785–86 by General Peleg Wadsworth, the writer's grandfather. The first brick house built in Portland (of Philadelphian bricks), its construction was delayed when inexperienced masons ran out of the unfamiliar building material. The third story and Federal roof were added in 1815. The Longfellows occupied the house in 1807, the year of the poet's birth, and Henry lived there until leaving for Bowdoin College in 1821. The site is today a museum operated by the Maine Historical Society.

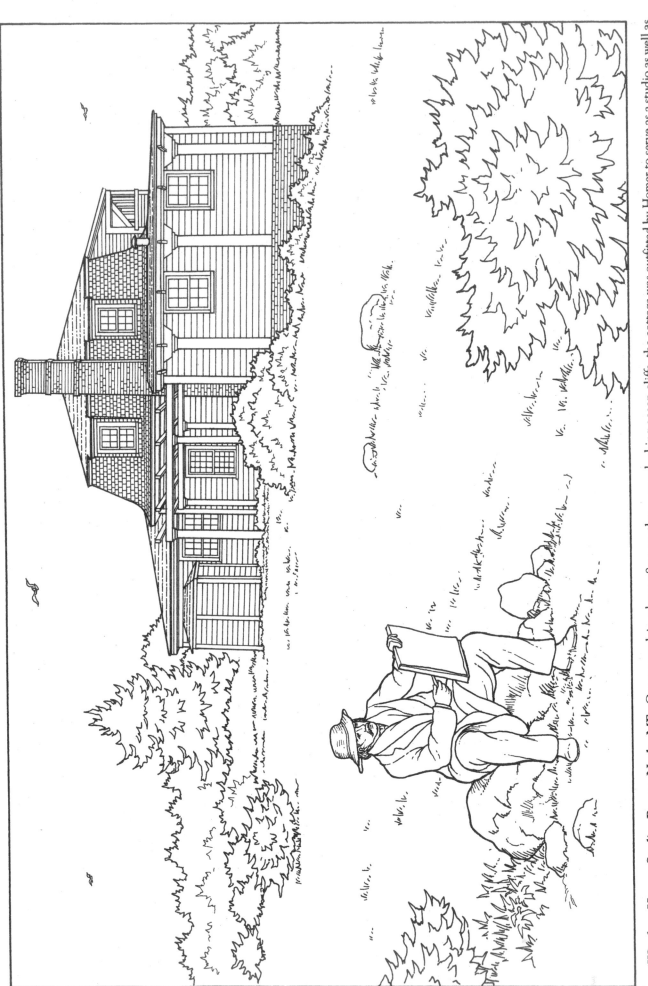

10  **Winslow Homer Studio, Prouts Neck, ME.** Constructed in about 1870 as the carriage house for a nearby home, this structure was moved and remodeled by Winslow Homer with the assistance of Maine architect John Calvin Stevens, and served as the artist's primary residence from 1884 until his death in 1910. Situated in a dramatic location overlooking ocean cliffs, the cottage was outfitted by Homer to serve as a studio as well as living space, and it was here that the artist created many of his famous works. Since Homer's death the studio has remained in his family's possession, and despite some remodeling appears much the same as it did in the artist's day.

**11 Sarah Orne Jewett House, South Berwick, ME.** Built in 1774, this handsome Georgian residence was already one of the area's showplaces when purchased by Captain Theodore Jewett in 1819. The wealthy seaman and shipbuilder outfitted the house with exotic goods from the world's ports. Today the house is celebrated primarily for its association with New England writer Sarah Orne Jewett, the captain's granddaughter, born here in 1849. The author, best known for her short fiction, excelled in her portrayals of the inhabitants and locales of the region. Today the house is maintained as the writer knew it by the Society for the Preservation of New England Antiquities.

**12  John Greenleaf Whittier Home, Amesbury, MA.** This early-nineteenth-century frame house was the permanent home of poet and abolitionist John Greenleaf Whittier from 1836 until his death in 1892. Whittier, still remembered for works such as "The Barefoot Boy" and *Snow-Bound*, enjoyed enormous success during his lifetime both as a popular poet and as an editor. A lifelong bachelor, the poet lived with family members, who shared his deep devotion to the Quaker faith. The house, which was enlarged from a modest cottage in 1847, has been maintained as a Whittier memorial since 1918, displaying family furnishings, manuscripts and the poet's study preserved as he left it.

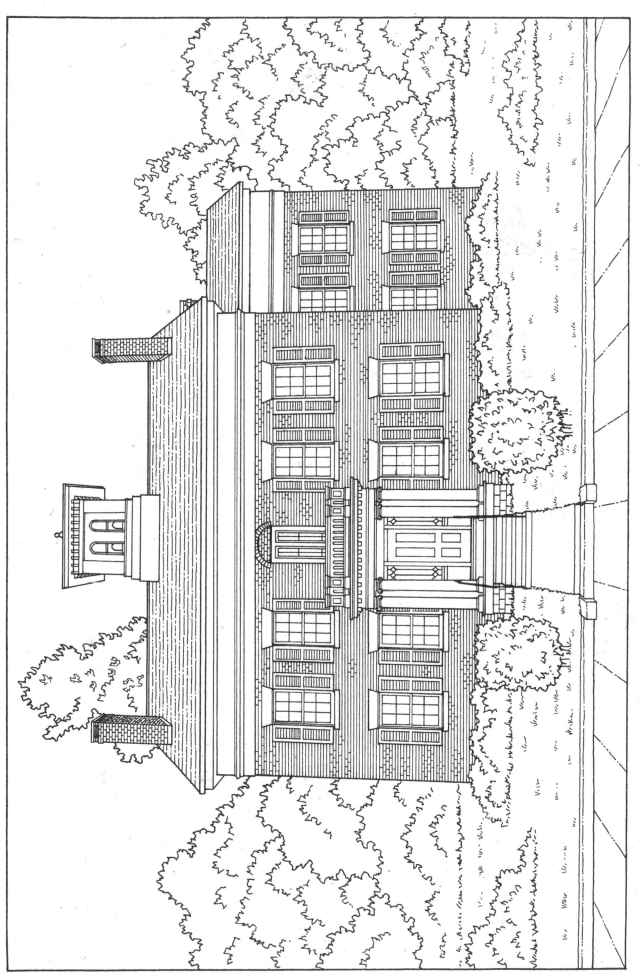

13　**Emily Dickinson Homestead, Amherst, MA.** This Federal style house was built in 1813 by Samuel Fowler Dickinson, a founder of nearby Amherst College. In 1830 Dickinson's granddaughter Emily was born in the house; she lived here with relatives all her life, except for a 15-year period when financial problems forced the family to move elsewhere. Emily Dickinson led a withdrawn existence, tending the garden and performing domestic tasks, and was considered something of an eccentric. After her death in 1886 the manuscripts of nearly 1800 poems, her life's work, were discovered. Today her home serves as a faculty residence for Amherst College, with occasional tours.

**14  Fenway Court (Isabella Stewart Gardner Museum), Boston, MA.** Home to one of the most distinguished private collections of art in the country, Fenway Court was the personal creation of Isabella Stewart Gardner, whose wealth and taste made possible the construction of a magnificent Venetian-style palazzo on Boston's newly filled Back Bay Fens between 1899 and 1902. Opened to the public in 1903, the structure also served as Ms. Gardner's residence until her death in 1924. Arranged precisely as she left them around a beautiful garden courtyard, the galleries display works by old masters as well as by contemporaries such as Gardner's friends James Abbott McNeill Whistler and John Singer Sargent.

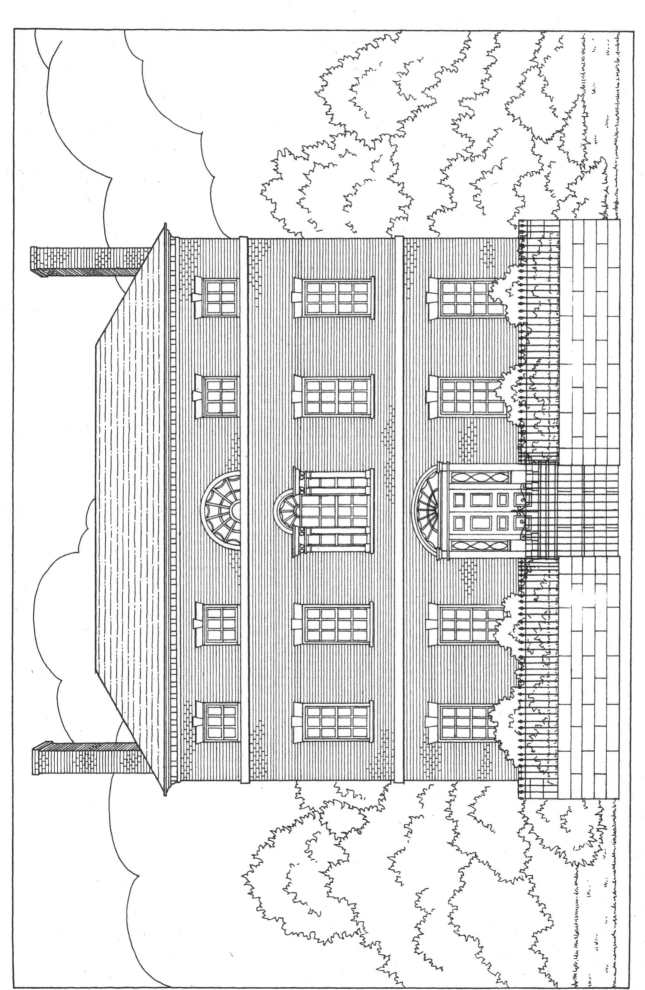

**15  Harrison Gray Otis House, Boston, MA.** The first (1796) of three houses designed by noted architect Charles Bulfinch for Federalist politician Harrison Gray Otis, this three-story brick structure epitomizes sophisticated urban architecture of the early republic. Otis, later a mayor of Boston, lived here only four years before moving his family to another Bulfinch dwelling on Beacon Hill. As the neighborhood decayed, the house was altered and adapted as a boarding house, its status when purchased by the Society for the Preservation of New England Antiquities in 1916. Painstakingly restored, the house today serves both as a museum and as headquarters to the Society.

**16 Paul Revere House, Boston, MA.** The only surviving seventeenth-century dwelling within the boundaries of old Boston, this house was constructed circa 1680 and initially served as the home of Robert Howard, a wealthy merchant. In 1770 it was purchased by Paul Revere, a silversmith and artisan who was to play a vital role in the coming War of Indepen-dence. Revere and his family occupied the house until 1800. The nineteenth century saw a decline in the fortunes of the area, and in 1905 the building, which had undergone many alterations, was scheduled for demolition. A campaign headed by Revere's great-grandson saved the structure, however, and the house was restored to its presumed original appearance.

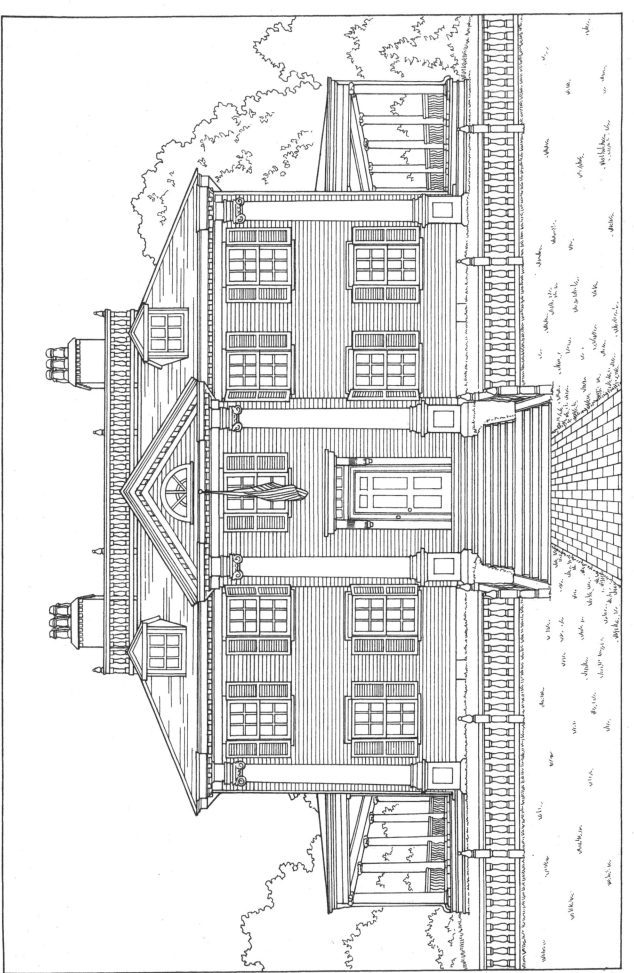

**17 Longfellow National Historic Site, Cambridge, MA.** Best known as the longtime abode of poet Henry Wadsworth Longfellow, this handsome mansion has enjoyed a colorful history since its construction in 1759 by a wealthy Tory. Abandoned by its owners during the Revolution, it served as a military hospital and as George Washington's headquarters during the siege of Boston. Longfellow first occupied the house as a boarder in 1837; it was later given to him by his bride's father. Here the poet lived until his death in 1882, writing works such as *The Song of Hiawatha* and *Evangeline*. Today the house, a museum, preserves Longfellow's furniture and effects.

18 **The Old Manse, Concord, MA.** The source of the title of Nathaniel Hawthorne's *Mosses from an Old Manse* (1846), a collection of short stories largely written here, The Old Manse was built by Reverend William Emerson circa 1770. Emerson's grandson, Transcendentalist Ralph Waldo Emerson, wrote his first book, *Nature*, while living here in 1834–35. From 1842 to 1845 the house was rented by Nathaniel Hawthorne and his wife, Sophia; the author gave the dwelling its picturesque name. Purchased from a descendant of Mrs. William Emerson in 1939 by The Trustees of Reservations, a nonprofit organization, the house has been restored and displays Concord literary memorabilia.

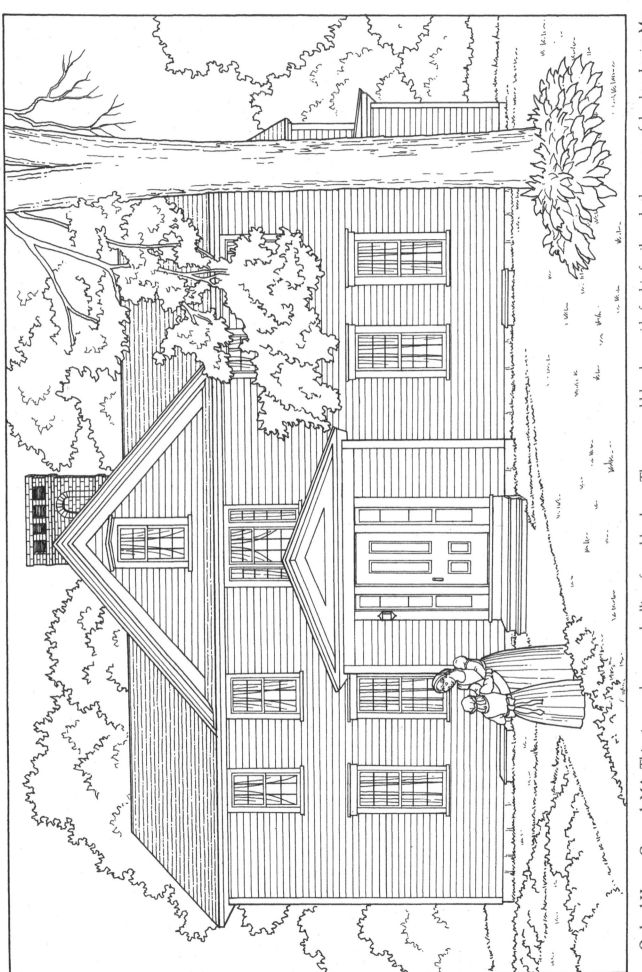

**19  Orchard House, Concord, MA.** This nineteenth-century dwelling, formed by the joining of two earlier structures, was home from 1858 until 1877 to the Alcotts, one of America's most illustrious literary dynasties. Family patriarch Bronson Alcott, although noted as a Transcendentalist philosopher and educator and an intimate of Emerson and Thoreau, could barely provide for his family; only the success of daughter Louisa May Alcott's autobiographical novel *Little Women*, written at Orchard House in 1868, rescued them from destitution. The success of that and subsequent writings by Ms. Alcott brought wealth to the family, whose humble abode is preserved today as a museum.

**20  William Cullen Bryant Homestead, Cummington, MA.** William Cullen Bryant, journalist and poet best remembered for "Thanatopsis" (written when he was seventeen), was born on this site in 1794, in a modest cabin that now makes up part of the second floor of this sprawling 23-room country house. The farm left family hands in 1835, but the author repurchased it thirty years later, expanding it to its present form. Here Bryant, after a distinguished career as editor of the *New-York Evening Post*, spent his final years enjoying nature while still immersed in literary matters. The house remains much as it did in Bryant's lifetime, and displays family furniture and effects.

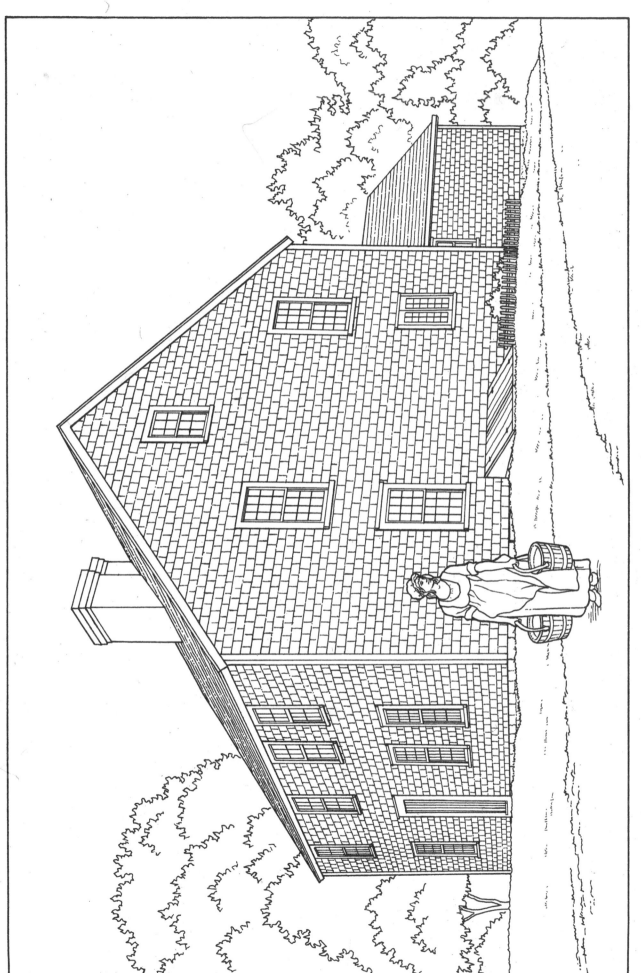

**21  John Alden House, Duxbury, MA.** This 1653 dwelling served as the later-life home of John and Priscilla Alden, the Pilgrim couple immortalized in Longfellow's poem "The Courtship of Miles Standish" (an almost wholly mythical account). John Alden sailed as a cooper on the *Mayflower* and helped found the Plymouth Colony before settling in nearby Duxbury circa 1627. The present structure was built by John and his sons to replace an earlier cottage (which was incorporated into the house). The rear extension was added in about 1820 by Alden's descendants. The last surviving signer of the Mayflower Compact, John Alden died at his home, today a museum, in 1687 at age eighty-eight.

**22  Beauport, Gloucester, MA.** One of the most eclectic dwellings in North America, Beauport was built to accommodate the manifold tastes of its owner/designer, the influential decorator Henry Davis Sleeper. Initially constructed in 1907 as a modest summer retreat, the house expanded over the following decades to total forty rooms at Sleeper's death in 1934. Beauport's eccentric exterior mirrors an interior designed as an amalgam of uniquely appointed rooms, filled with rare antiques and decorative items. Today maintained as a museum by the Society for the Preservation of New England Antiquities, Beauport preserves Sleeper's showplace much as he left it.

**23   The Mount, Lenox, MA.** The summer home of author Edith Wharton from 1902 until 1911, this 35-room "cottage" reflects the classical precepts of architecture and design adopted by the writer after extensive study of European models. The fifty acres of grounds were landscaped by Wharton in consultation with her niece, noted landscape designer Beatrix Farrand, and include elaborate gardens. While living here the author wrote many works, including *The House of Mirth* (1905), and entertained such notables as her friend and literary mentor Henry James. Today the estate is being renovated under the auspices of the Edith Wharton Restoration, Inc., which offers tours.

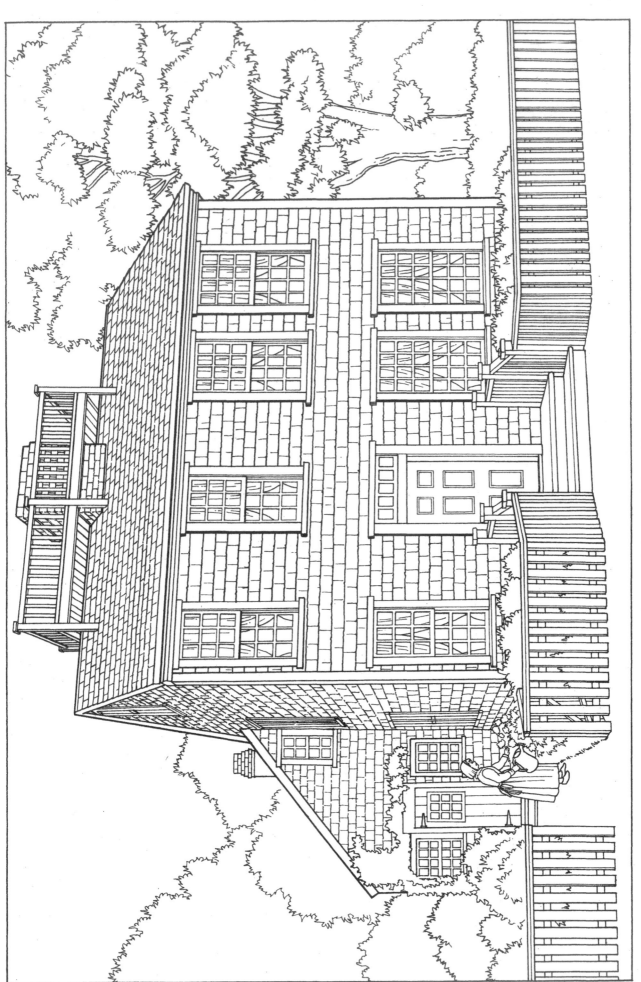

**24** **Maria Mitchell Birthplace, Nantucket, MA.** Built in 1790, this typical Quaker house was for years home of America's first celebrated female astronomer, born here in 1818. An assistant from childhood to her father, an amateur astronomer, Maria Mitchell became internationally famous following her 1847 discovery of a new comet, which she charted from atop a Nantucket bank. In later years she taught astronomy at Vassar College. After Mitchell's death in 1889 the birthplace was acquired by a memorial association, and over the years the site has been expanded into both a house museum containing family artifacts (including Mitchell's telescopes) and an educational science center.

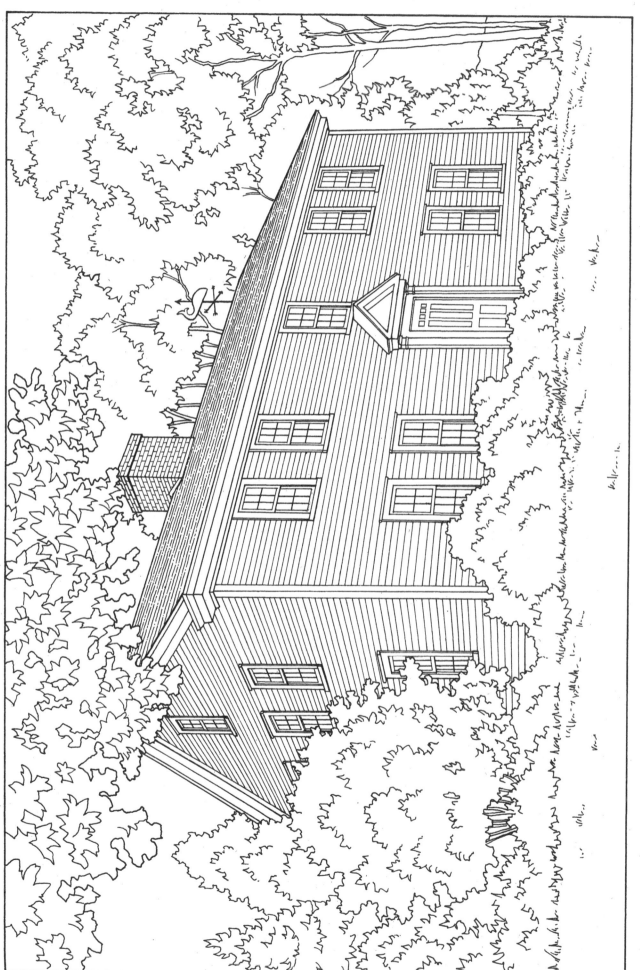

**25  Arrowhead, Pittsfield, MA.** This eighteenth-century farmhouse was purchased in 1850 by author Herman Melville, who wished to escape the noise and turmoil of New York. Melville lived here for thirteen years, completing *Moby-Dick* and composing masterpieces such as *Pierre* and the stories collected in *The Piazza Tales*. This period, despite its productivity and Melville's influential friendship with neighbor Nathaniel Hawthorne, was overshadowed by financial woes, depression and popular rejection. Operated by the Berkshire County Historical Society, the house and an adjoining barn in which Melville and Hawthorne discussed their art are now preserved as a literary shrine.

**26 Adams National Historic Site, Quincy, MA.** Constructed in 1731 by Leonard Vassall, a sugar planter from Jamaica, this large clapboard house was home from 1788 to 1927 to four generations of the distinguished Adams family, including Presidents John and John Quincy Adams, First Lady Abigail Adams and author Henry Adams. Named "Peacefield" by the second President, the house was enlarged over the years as the family's size and wealth increased, and a massive granite library was erected on the site to preserve historic books and documents. Family furniture and effects have also been scrupulously maintained at the site, which was presented to the U.S. Government in 1946.

**27** **House of the Seven Gables, Salem, MA.** Immortalized in Nathaniel Hawthorne's 1851 novel of the same name, the House of the Seven Gables has come to symbolize the colorful history of early Salem. Originally the four-gabled 1668 home of Captain John Turner, the house had gained three gables by the mid-nineteenth century, when it was occupied by Hawthorne's cousin Susannah Ingersoll. The author, a frequent guest, was inspired to write his romance by the dwelling's curious form, by local legends recounted by his cousin and by his own Puritan ancestry. Restored early in the twentieth century, the house operates as a museum displaying period artifacts and Hawthorniana.

**28  Thornton W. Burgess Museum, Sandwich, MA.** Situated in the center of Sandwich, the first town settled on Cape Cod, this house-museum memorializes Thornton W. Burgess, the naturalist and prolific children's author best known for whimsical yet informative tales of woodland creatures such as *The Adventures of Peter Cottontail*. The Colonial dwelling—formerly the home of Burgess' aunt—exhibits material relating to the author and to the natural history of Cape Cod. Maintained by the Thornton W. Burgess Society, which also operates the Burgess-oriented Green Briar Nature Center nearby, the museum offers live-animal storytimes during the summer months.

**29 Chesterwood, Stockbridge, MA.** A Berkshire farm transformed into an artist's summer estate, Chesterwood was a seasonal living and working place for sculptor Daniel Chester French from 1897 until his death in 1931. Best known for the seated *Abraham Lincoln* in the Lincoln Memorial in Washington, D.C., French commissioned the Memorial's architect, his friend Henry Bacon, to design the main house of the compound. The site also features an attractive studio (shown) and a gallery for the sculptor's work, converted from a barn. Donated to the National Trust for Historic Preservation in 1969 by French's daughter, Chesterwood preserves a beautiful artistic retreat.

**30 Augustus Saint-Gaudens National Historic Site (Aspet House), Cornish, NH.** The frequent home of noted sculptor Augustus Saint Gaudens from 1885 until his death in 1907, this Federal brick structure, once an inn, was built circa 1800. Renovated by the artist to serve as a working as well as living location, the estate includes studios and gardens constructed to his own specifications. Saint Gaudens' move to Cornish initiated an artists' colony in the region that attracted notables of the day, and it was here that he completed many of his most famous works. A National Historic Site since 1965, the grounds display the sculptor's work and effects, as well as his tomb.

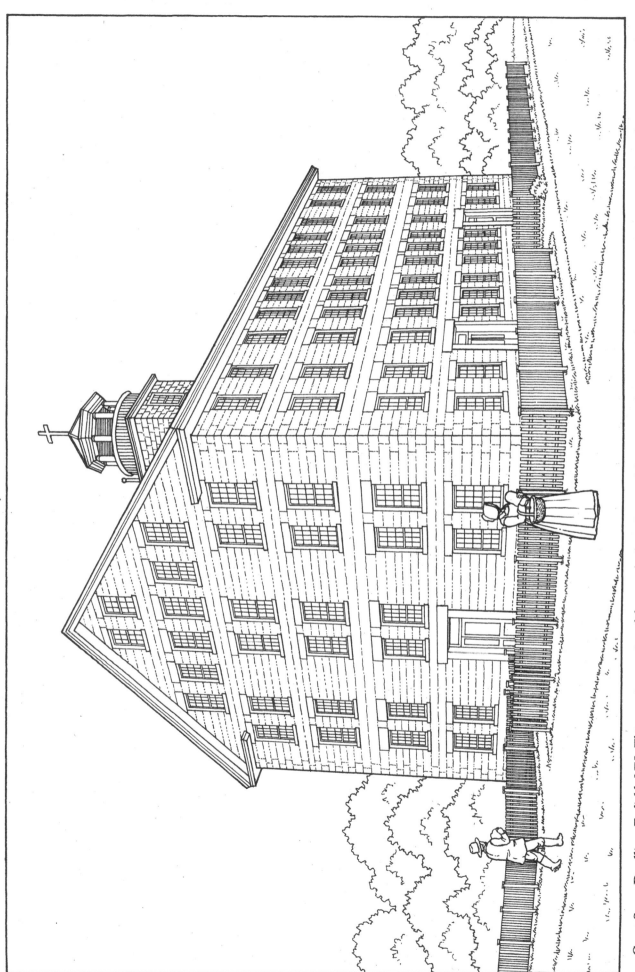

**31  Great Stone Dwelling, Enfield, NH.** This massive granite edifice was built as the living quarters for about 150 members of the Church Family of the local Shaker community. The Shakers, a millenarian sect founded during the Revolutionary War, practiced strict doctrines of celibacy and asceticism, peaking in popularity during the second quarter of the nineteenth century. The Great Stone Dwelling was built between 1837 and 1841 to the specifications of local architect Ammi Burnham Young. A decline in numbers forced the sect to sell the village in 1923; sixty years later, it was opened as a museum devoted to the lifestyle and handicrafts of the group.

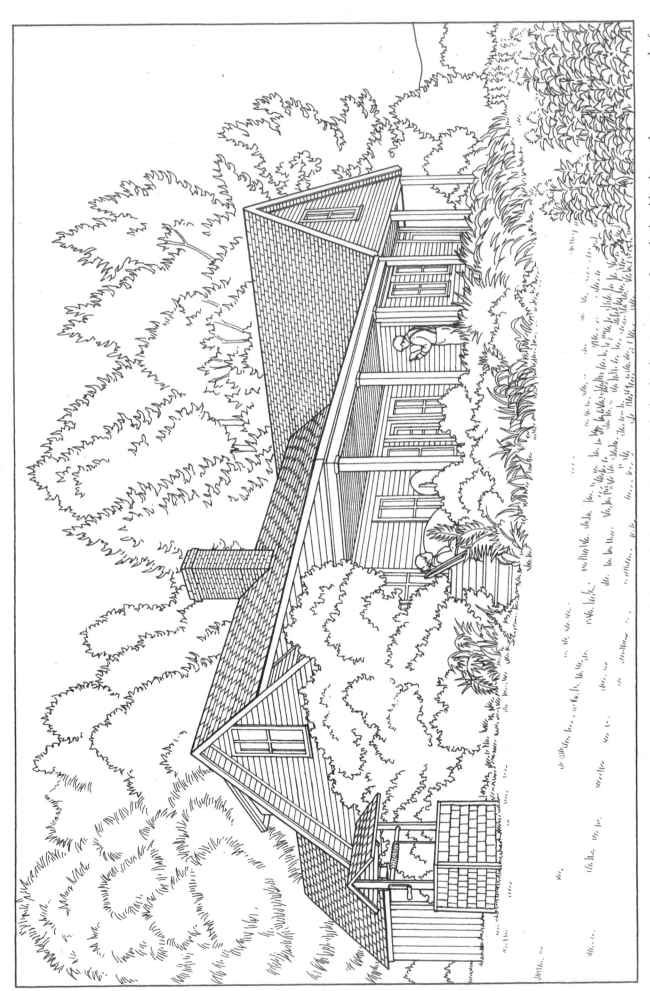

**32  Robert Frost Place, Franconia, NH.** Poet Robert Frost occupied this simple farmhouse from 1915 to 1920, a period that saw his transformation from a virtual unknown into one of the most successful and distinctive voices on the poetry scene. Those years saw the composition of works such as "The Road Not Taken" and "Stopping by Woods on a Snowy Evening," which take their inspiration from the local landscape. In recent years the farm has been purchased by the Town of Franconia and transformed into a center for poetry and the arts, featuring a museum and a poetry and nature trail, adorned with Frost's verse. Regular programs include readings and an annual poetry festival.

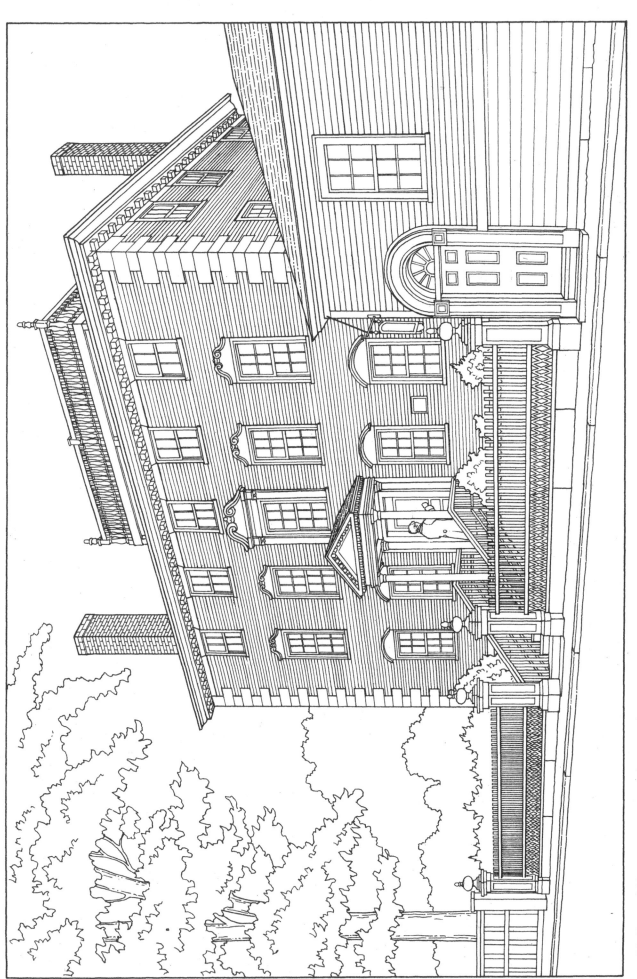

**33 Moffatt–Ladd House, Portsmouth, NH.** This imposing Georgian mansion, one of the earliest three-story residences in the region, was built in 1763 by Captain John Moffatt as a wedding gift for his son, Samuel. Kept in family hands until opened as a museum in 1913, the house is one of the most extensively documented Colonial dwellings, with two surviving eighteenth-century inventories detailing its original décor and contents. Maintained by the National Society of the Colonial Dames of America in the State of New Hampshire, the site includes a nineteenth-century counting house and garden, as well as a horse chestnut planted in 1776 by a signer of the Declaration of Independence.

**34** **The Breakers, Newport, RI.** Designed by Richard Morris Hunt, The Breakers was built between 1893 and 1895 by tycoon Cornelius Vanderbilt II to replace a previous mansion of the same name that burned in 1892. The lavish summer "cottage" was modeled on Italian Renaissance villas and cost some $7,000,000 to construct. Considered the most opulent mansion of an age of opulence, The Breakers witnessed brilliant gala parties for the nation's wealthiest. The impressive grounds, landscaped by the firm of Frederick Law Olmsted, include luxurious stables. Still partially occupied by Vanderbilt scions, the house is open for tours given by the Preservation Society of Newport County.

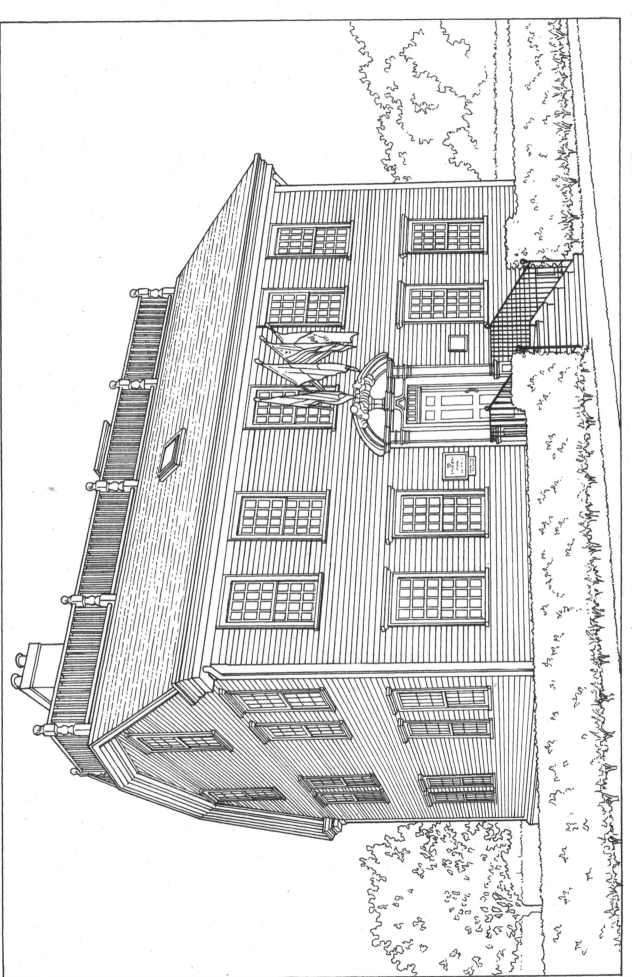

**35  Hunter House, Newport, RI.** A relic of Newport's early history as an important Colonial port, Hunter House ranks among America's most attractive surviving eighteenth-century residences. Built in 1748, when Newport surpassed both New York and Boston in sea trade, the structure was initially home to Deputy Governor Jonathan Nichols; after a succession of occupants it was purchased in 1805 by lawyer William R. Hunter, who owned it for nearly fifty years. Later altered for use as a boarding house and convalescent home, the site was acquired by the Preservation Society of Newport County in 1945 and subsequently restored as a museum replete with period furnishings.

36 **Kingscote, Newport, RI.** This charming Gothic Revival villa was constructed in 1839 by a summer resident from Savannah. Designed by Richard Upjohn, an architect best known for his churches (including Trinity Church in New York City), the structure mirrors contemporary trends toward integration of dwelling and site. The house was expanded in 1881 under the supervision of Stanford White, who created a spectacular dining room featuring a wall of Tiffany glass. The first of Newport's sumptuous summer cottages, Kingscote pointed the way for the opulent mansions that followed. Today the house is a museum operated by the Preservation Society of Newport County.

37 **John Brown House, Providence, RI.** Named after prosperous merchant John Brown, this 1786 brick mansion elegantly reflects its builder's wealth and status. Brown's brother Joseph designed the house, which achieved immediate acclaim as one of the premier residences in the newly independent nation. Here Brown and his family entertained such luminaries as George Washington and Thomas Jefferson, whose cause they had championed during the Revolution. Later occupants, including Providence magnate Marsden Perry, preserved the site's Early American flair. Today the house is home to the Rhode Island Historical Society, and displays family and period items.

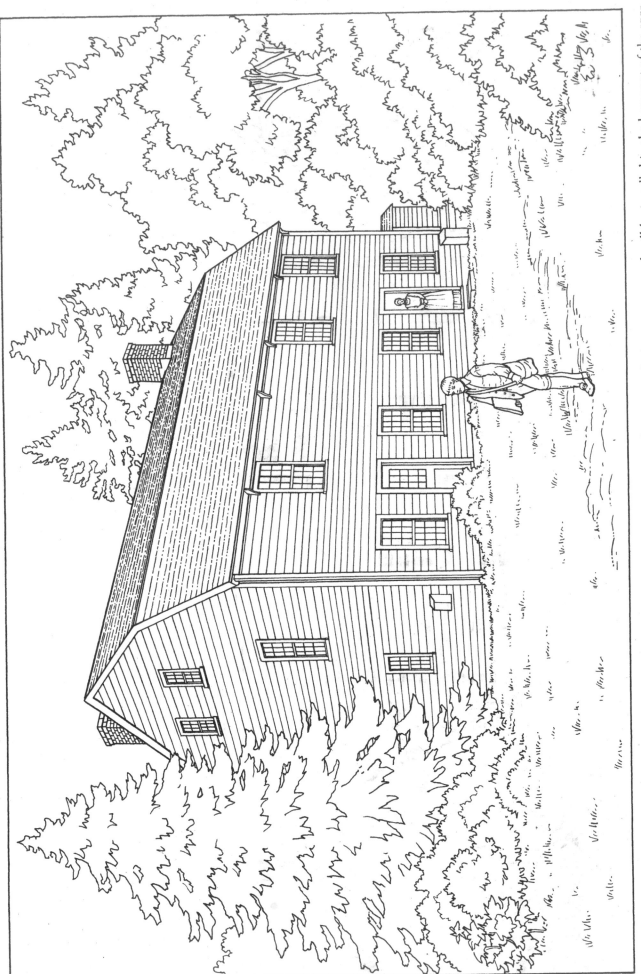

**38  Gilbert Stuart Birthplace, Saunderstown, RI.** This gambrel-roofed house is significant both as the natal home of painter Gilbert Stuart, whose familiar portrait of George Washington still adorns schoolrooms, and as the site of the first working snuff mill in America. Stuart's father, a Scottish immigrant, made his living grinding snuff for New England's gentry with the water-powered mill he installed in the basement of the 1751 family home. The artist, born here in 1755, lived in Rhode Island until leaving to study painting in England. Maintained since 1930 by the Gilbert Stuart Memorial, Inc., the restored house features a working replica of the historic mill.

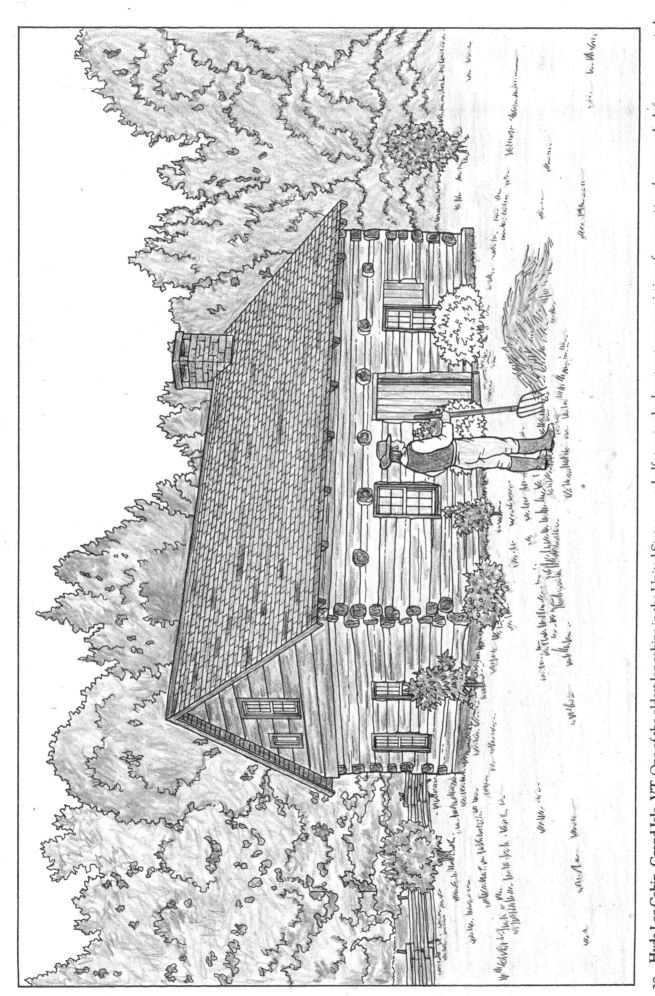

39 **Hyde Log Cabin, Grand Isle, VT.** One of the oldest log cabins in the United States, this building was constructed circa 1783 by Jedediah Hyde, Jr., on land purchased by his father from veterans of Ethan Allen's Green Mountain Boys. Hyde, who had served in the Revolution, surveyed Grand Isle and other parts of Vermont with his father. The one-and-a-half story cedar log structure, consisting of one 20 × 25′ room and a loft, was occupied by members of Hyde's family for nearly 150 years. Today the cabin, which has been moved two miles from its original site, is operated as a museum displaying historic maps, furniture and other period items by the state.

**40  Hildene (Robert Todd Lincoln House), Manchester, VT.** A 24-room Georgian Revival mansion, Hildene was built in 1904 as the summer home of Robert Todd Lincoln, the only child of Abraham Lincoln who lived to adulthood. Designed by the Boston architectural firm of Shepley, Rutan, and Coolidge, the house has remained remarkably well preserved, maintaining many original furnishings, family items and an unusual player organ. Lincoln, a former statesman and executive of the Pullman Company (which he advised during its notorious strike), occupied the site until his death in 1926. The estate remained in family hands until the 1970s; today, restored, it serves as a museum.

**41 Emma Willard House, Middlebury, VT.** In this house in 1814 educator Emma Willard opened the Middlebury Female Seminary, a pioneering private institution for the instruction of young women in serious academic subjects (previously, women's higher education had focused primarily on tokens of breeding such as French and singing). Willard, born in Connecticut in 1787, came to Middlebury in 1807 to assume a teaching position. This L-shaped Federal brick structure was built in 1809 and served as Willard's home after her marriage that year to physician John Willard. Today the house serves as the admissions office for Middlebury College, and is open by appointment.

**42  Park–McCullough House, North Bennington, VT.** One of the finest examples of Second Empire architecture in New England, this 35-room Victorian mansion has been home to two Vermont governors. Constructed in 1865 as a summer home for Trenor Park, a local lawyer who had amassed a fortune managing John C. Frémont's Mariposa gold mines in California, the house was designed by the New York firm of Diaper and Dudley. For over 100 years the site was occupied by Park's relatives and descendants, who carefully maintained its lavish interior and furnishings. Today the house, operated as a museum, preserves an unusually complete record of a vanished way of life.

**43  Coolidge Homestead, Plymouth Notch, VT.** In this sprawling farmhouse, by the light of a kerosene lamp, Calvin Coolidge was sworn in as the thirtieth U.S. President by his father, a notary public, at 2:47 A.M. on August 3, 1923. This unusual ceremony, occurred after news of President Warren G. Harding's sudden death reached the vacationing Vice President at his boyhood home. Today maintained as it appeared at that historic moment, the nineteenth-century dwelling preserves the furniture and effects of the Coolidge family, who occupied it in 1876, when Calvin was four years old. The house's barn is attached to the main dwelling, allowing convenient access during Vermont winters.